MW01232063

Annabelle's Best Summer Ever

by

Rhonda Atkins Leonard

This book
belongs to:

_____

_____

Given by:

_____

Date: _____

Occasion:

_____

Written and illustrated by
Rhonda Atkins Leonard.
annabellestore.com
cogloamigos.com

The artist used scanned watercolors to
create the illustrations.

CoGlo Amigos and Annabelle are
trademarks of Color Glory, LLC.
Text copyright ©2021
Illustrations copyright ©2021

ISBN 978-1-304-60266-4

I hope Annabelle the colorful
giraffe and the CoGlo Amigos™
brighten all of your days!

Many thanks to
Bärbel H. Amos, my art instructor,
for sharing her talent and vision!

Thanks to the ELYSIAN team
for their partnership in publishing
and production.

And finally, thanks to J&D Photo
in Greenville, SC for all the help,
including professional scanning.
-Rhonda

Annabelle's Best Summer Ever

by
Rhonda
Atkins
Leonard

Annabelle had a great spring. In fact, it was her Best Spring Ever!

But as balloons floated by, she got the feeling that her summer fun was about to begin!

It was a warm, sunny day, so she put on her roller skates and headed to the park.

Along the way
she stopped
to get an
ice cream.

Then she heard
the laughter
of her good
friend Barboo
the balloon man.

Annabelle loved
the funny hats
Barboo made
for her.

Fun, fun, summer fun!

After spending time in the park, Annabelle returned home.

She planned a sleepover with her friends— Glory the zebra and Mingo Rose the elephant!

The three friends were thrilled to spend time together. They talked, laughed and blew bubbles for hours.

Backyard camping
under the stars

was the perfect end
to a wonderful day.

Zzzz.

Zzzz.

Zzzz.

They counted the fireflies

as they danced about.

Summer flew by with one adventure after another.

Now she was excited
to see what treasures
fall would bring.

THE END

Thanks for reading!

Follow Annabelle's journeys in "Annabelle's Best Fall Ever"!

There were sunny days . . .

and holidays . . .

. . . lazy days,

. . . and crazy days.

And . . . there were days at the beach!

Then it was
time to go home.

Wherever Annabelle's travels took her, home was always her favorite place.

So when the cool breezes of September announced summer's end, Annabelle knew without a doubt that it had been her Best Summer Ever!

Always
be your
best!

Collect all the CoGlo Amigos™ books!